The Stolen Treasure of Mammoth Cave

Steve Kistler

Cover art and illustrations by John Yakel

authorHOUSE®

AuthorHouse™
1663 Liberty Drive
Bloomington, IN 47403
www.authorhouse.com
Phone: 1-800-839-8640

Published by AuthorHouse   9/11/12

ISBN: 978-1-4772-6247-4 (sc)
ISBN: 978-1-4772-6388-4 (e)

This book is printed on acid-free paper.

Also by Steve Kistler

The Mystery of Mammoth Cave

Acknowledgements

I would like to thank my editors, Sue and Janet, for their hard work and support.

Chapter I

James knew he was in trouble as soon as the river water touched his legs.

Ooohh, that's cold!!

He tried to tip the capsizing canoe back the other way and was greeted by a new wave washing in from the opposite side. It completely covered his lower half, as the canoe went under.

Arggh! I can't believe...

Finally his mouth formed words. "Uncle Richard, help me! Help!!"

His uncle was so busy laughing that he almost tipped his own boat into the drink. "Not much I can do for you now, good buddy" he roared. "Don't worry, it's shallow here."

James hadn't noticed that the Green River was only a few feet deep at this point. *Just enough to get totally soaked in a canoe*, he thought. Getting over the shock to his system from the unexpected bath, the boy climbed out of the sunken boat and stood up. The water came to just above his knees.

"Don't worry James, it happens to everyone." He knew Aunt Courtney was just trying to be nice, but he was glad for her kindness. "We've all gone in the river at one time or another."

In an odd way, it felt better to know that. It had happened so fast; one minute he was leaning to his left looking at the water, and the next he was up to his belly button in cold water. A fine way to spend his first afternoon back in Kentucky!

"I think we've had enough for today," said his uncle. "What do you say we head back to the house and find some dry clothes for you?"

It was a warm October afternoon, but James was still chilly from his sudden immersion. "Sounds good to me. Sorry I messed up."

"You didn't mess up at all, James. Courtney told you the truth when she said we've both been in the river before. Canoes are tippy boats. Next time you'll know better."

Back in Kentucky! There were few places the boy loved as much as Mammoth Cave National Park, and having an aunt and uncle who worked there sure helped.

As the staff ecologist, Uncle Richard was the chief organizer of a conference on Native Peoples being held there this week. He had called James's parents two weeks earlier to invite his nephew to Kentucky for the event. Much to James's surprise, his parents had agreed to let him travel to his relatives' home on his own for the week.

As James dragged his sunken canoe out of the water, he saw a large bird soar overhead.

"Wow!" Aunt Courtney spoke. "A bald eagle, James! They

have a nest on the river and we get to see them once in a while. What a lucky day!"

As if to emphasize the point, another huge bird came flying toward them about thirty feet above the water. The boaters remained motionless as they watched the powerful raptor fly over. James could see the white head and tail perfectly; each feather seemed to stand out in the clear fall sunlight.

"Amazing!" Uncle Richard spoke what they were all feeling.

Boy, a lot's happening already and it's only my first day back. I'll have to be sure to tell Mom and Dad everything, James mused. *Good thing I brought my journal.*

The party pulled their canoes out of the water at the Green River Ferry landing. James noticed several cars in the Echo River parking lot.

"What's up that way?" he inquired, pointing to a trailhead.

"That's the Echo River Spring trail. It leads to a spot where the Echo River bubbles out of the cave." Richard answered. "I'd be glad to take you up there, but right now I need to go deal with last minute preparations for our conference. Tomorrow morning we have cave trips for our visiting archaeologists, and after lunch we'll have sessions where they present their research papers. You may not be able to understand all of them, but I think you'll enjoy hearing about their work."

"By the way, I have some dry clothes in the car. Just hide behind the open door and you can change."

His uncle's pants and shirt were comically large, but they were dry. James opened the car door to give himself a screen, then stripped out of his wet duds. Rolling up the pants legs and shirt sleeves, he found that they would make do nicely until they got back home.

Driving up the hill to the visitor center, Aunt Courtney spoke again. "I've been saving a surprise for you, James, mostly because I wasn't sure it would work out. It looks like a friend of yours will be here this week, too."

"*Shanda's* here??!?" James could barely believe what he was hearing. Shanda was a girl he'd met last summer at the park; she and James had teamed up to solve a mystery that had been plaguing local historians for more than a century. However, the fact that they snuck into the cave to do so had resulted in their being banned from going back in for the remainder of their visit. James was secretly hoping to be allowed to join the archaeologists on their trip tomorrow, but he hadn't raised the subject yet with his aunt and uncle.

"Where is she? When can we see her?" All of a sudden, he was excited to see his partner in adventure. Shanda was the coolest girl James had ever met. She was smart, friendly, and hilarious. She took special delight in teasing James for the dumb things he occasionally said, but she was so funny that he wasn't offended. In fact, he was usually laughing right along with her.

"I think her uncle Matthew's working this afternoon," Aunt

Courtney continued as they pulled into the parking lot. "Let's go take a look around the visitors center."

As she spoke, James scanned the area for anyone he knew. He had met several of the rangers the previous summer, and he hoped maybe he could spot someone he recognized.

"Look James," Courtney spoke up. "That sure didn't take long."

Coming out of the visitor center doors were a tall man and a thirteen-year-old girl.

Ranger Matthew and Shanda! James could hardly contain himself. He barely waited for his uncle to stop the car; then he hopped out and ran toward them. As he drew closer, he could see that Shanda had grown taller in the few months since they'd been together. She didn't look as chubby as she had last summer. In fact, she looked more like...a girl.

Shanda turned at the sound of his footsteps and actually squealed at the sight of him running toward her. *What now*, thought James, *do I shake her hand?* It seemed a little personal to hug this girl he had only known for one week last June.

Shanda solved the problem by grabbing him in a bear hug and twirling him right off his feet in a big circle. "Howdy, cowboy!" she screamed, almost in his ear. "I'm so glad you're here, but you sure haven't gotten any prettier since last year. I'm staying in Tennessee; you Ohio dudes are *ugly*." Laughing together, they separated and had a good look at each other. *This is going to be a lot easier than I thought,* James realized.

"Hello, James. It's great to see you again."

In his excitement to see Shanda, James had momentarily forgotten about Ranger Matthew. Shanda's uncle was a quiet, friendly man; James had liked him from their first meeting. Aunt Courtney had explained how Matthew and Shanda were both descended from the early slave guides at Mammoth Cave who had been brought to the park in the late 1830's.

"Ranger Matthew! It sure is good to see you again, too," he enthused.

After the initial excitement of their reunion wore off a little, James and Shanda started catching up about school and whatever else was going on in their lives. Uncle Richard and Aunt Courtney came over and joined them.

"Hello, Matthew." Richard spoke. "Beautiful day."

"It is that. You all ready for the big conference?"

"As ready as I'll ever be. I wouldn't say it's big; we have twenty-eight participants. But they are among the leading archaeologists in the country, so I'm pleased."

"Matthew," Aunt Courtney spoke up. "Would you and Shanda like to join us for supper? It won't be anything fancy, but we'd love to have you."

"I won't be able to; I've got church tonight. But Shanda might like to join you if you can tolerate her."

They looked at the two teenagers, who were nodding their heads in unison.

"Looks like that's settled." Aunt Courtney smiled. "How about if I drop her back at your place after supper?"

"No need to do that. I'll swing by on my way home. Shanda, if you don't behave, I'll slap you back to last Tuesday."

Shanda laughed out loud, knowing that her uncle would never slap her under any circumstances. "OK, Uncle Matthew. If I can steal some silverware, I'll split it with you."

Something about having Shanda around put James's brain in low gear. She was too quick. *No problem for me*, he thought. *I still get to hang out with her.*

The foursome drove to Richard and Courtney's house right outside the park, with the two kids chattering like squirrels all the way home.

*****

About the time James and Shanda were reuniting in the parking lot, two men were registering at the park hotel. One was tall, standing a good six foot two. His most noticeable feature was his long, fiery red hair. His companion was remarkably unremarkable: brown hair, hazel eyes, and a little chubby through the waist. Both looked to be in their early forties.

"Got the list and the duffel bag?" Red asked his partner.

"Of course. Quit being so nervous. We've got it all lined up."

"I know, I know. It's just that I don't see us getting another chance like this one ever again."

"You're right, but don't worry. We've planned too carefully to fail now."

"Two days from now our working days will be over."

The two visitors took their room keys and went to search for the conference registration desk.

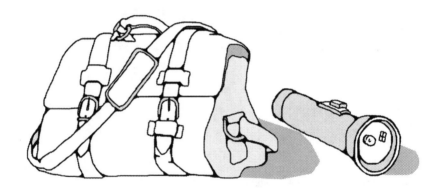

Chapter II

That evening, Aunt Courtney served late potatoes from their garden, along with summer beans and corn from the freezer. Uncle Richard fired up the grill and put some marinated pork ribs on the flames. The aroma of the cooking meat made James's mouth water, and when he actually took his first bite he was tempted to stand up and crow like a rooster!

"This is the best food I've ever had!" he told his aunt and uncle.

Shanda just grinned her agreement, as her mouth was full of potatoes at the moment.

"Thanks, guys," Uncle Richard replied. "We have a young man nearby who raises organic grass-fed meat. I have to agree with you; it's the best we've ever had too."

After a few minutes, Aunt Courtney changed the subject. "How's your school year going, you two? Seventh grade can be a big adjustment."

"Mine's OK," James allowed. "I've got good teachers,

especially Ms. Robertson in math. She makes it fun, and I love graphing."

"I moved to a new school this time," Shanda spoke up.

Oh, no, thought James. *I hope she didn't get kicked out of the last one.* Shanda had had a few problems at her former school for playing too many practical jokes on her principal and teachers.

Shanda must have read the concern in his face. "I wasn't forced to move, James. Our middle school has seventh and eighth grades in it, so it was time to move up. That gives me plenty of new opportunities, though." She smiled her devilish smile.

I'd love to be in a class with her, thought James. *She's always up to something.*

"Actually, the year's just started," Shanda continued. "But we have an assistant principal who's getting on everyone's nerves a little bit. There was no need for her to be a Nazi on the first day!"

"Shanda, I'm sure the lady is just doing her best under trying conditions," Aunt Courtney commented. "Try to get to know her a little; I'm sure she'll turn out to be OK."

"Well, I don't do drugs, and my friends don't either. I hate the way she looks at us like we're all gang members, ready to slit her throat. My best friend, Jacquie, gets all A's, and she's been called in for random locker searches three times already this year." She stopped to take a breath. "Sorry. I get worked up too easily over the dragon lady. Jacquie's only crime is guilt by association," she smirked. "She hangs out with me too much."

"I'm sure everything will smooth out as they get to know you, Shanda. Everyone here at the park is always glad to have you visit your uncle."

"Well, I did prepare a couple of surprises for dragon lady," Shanda smiled as she continued. "I didn't exactly leave my name behind, though."

Uh-oh. This sounds like the dollar bill trick she played on her last principal, James thought.

Shanda read his thoughts again. "Actually, James, we're getting more creative." As she spoke, she started to laugh quietly to herself. "A few weeks ago, we had a guest speaker who showed us the effects of liquid nitrogen. Did you know you can freeze a flower in that stuff for ten seconds and it will shatter like glass? It was amazing. He said it's colder than 300 degrees below zero!"

"Anyway, I found this great trick online. You know those canisters of shaving cream you can get at the drug store? Well, we took four of those and froze them in liquid nitrogen." Shanda's eyes shone as she remembered the day. "After they solidified, one of my friends took a sharp knife and removed the cardboard containers, so we just had chunks of solid shaving cream." She started chuckling again.

"Then..." she could hardly get the words out as she broke out laughing. "We slipped them inside her car window in the parking lot! She always leaves her windows open a little for ventilation."

"Oh, no!" Uncle Richard exclaimed. "That's really devious!"

Courtney and James both looked puzzled. It was James who spoke next.

"What happened then, Shanda?"

"As they heated up, they expanded. Her car actually filled up with shaving cream! You should have seen it…" The girl was laughing so hard now that tears were rolling down her face. "It was foaming out all the windows. The whole car was one big sudsy mess!"

Despite their misgivings, her three listeners were guffawing right along with her. The image of the car overflowing with shaving cream was too much. As they realized what Shanda and her friends had pulled off, they roared with laughter.

"Shanda, that's pure genius!" James exclaimed. "You have definitely stepped it up a notch since last year."

As she got herself under control, Shanda spoke to Uncle Richard and Aunt Courtney. "I would never hurt anyone, believe me. I know the difference between right and wrong; I just don't like to let people walk on me and my friends."

"Anyway," she continued, "the dragon lady seems to have settled down a bit. If she looks my way again I may need to send her another reminder of how to treat people."

The other three waited, almost afraid to ask what she had in mind next.

"No big deal," Shanda said. "It might involve some extra strength double-sided tape and a toilet seat in the office restroom."

"Shanda, you wouldn't!" Aunt Courtney looked genuinely concerned. " Please, honey, don't take this too far. The last thing you want to do is get branded as a troublemaker and ruin your chances at a good education."

"I know you're right, and I won't do anything too stupid, believe me. But a girl can always dream, right?"

They chatted for another half hour about school and about their adventures of the previous summer. Both kids had been local celebrities for a month or so after their big discovery in the cave. James had appeared on several local TV shows, and he and Shanda had actually been guests on a famous national talk show.

When Shanda's uncle returned, they were in a jovial mood, trading jokes and tall tales for their own amusement. Shanda was just finishing up a wild tale of how she and two friends had stenciled handicapped symbols in every parking space in the school lot. James had no idea how true it all was, but it didn't matter. She could read the phone book and sound hilarious.

As Ranger Matthew joined them, Aunt Courtney served home-made apple pie and ice cream. *Wow,* thought James, *I could get used to eating like this all the time.*

"So," Uncle Richard spoke. "Do either of you want to join the archaeologists' trip tomorrow? We'll be exploring parts of the cave which most visitors never get to see."

James and Shanda both answered quickly, as if they were afraid that Richard would withdraw his offer if they hesitated. "You bet." "Yes sir."

"I thought you might." Uncle Richard's eyes smiled as he spoke. "Great. Matthew, if it suits your schedule, can we meet about 9:00 at the conference center?"

"That would fit my schedule perfectly, Richard. Can you keep an eye on Shanda for me? She's been known to let her imagination run at times."

"Well, that's hard to believe." Richard spoke with a straight face while the girl beside him smiled innocently. "But we'll be sure she toes the line tomorrow."

Then Shanda and Matthew thanked their hosts for the

wonderful food and bid them good night. The happy group broke up with promises to meet again the next morning.

*****

A few miles away, in a hotel room at the park, two archaeologists studied a cave map.

The tall man with the red hair was speaking. "Our best chance for finding the good stuff will be in Blackall Avenue. I was in there once, about three years ago. If we get a chance, we'll go take a look around tomorrow."

"Sounds good to me," his partner replied. "I've been looking forward to this payday for a long time."

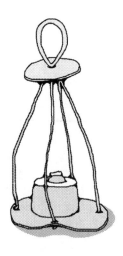

Chapter III

Sunday morning dawned like a clear blue stream in the valley where Richard and Courtney lived. James found them out on the porch, eating fruit salad and drinking tea in the cool fall air. At six feet and two inches, Richard looked cool in his green and gray park uniform. His dark, curly hair was still wet from his morning shower.

Aunt Courtney was almost as tall as his uncle; she beamed at James as he came out on the porch.

"Good morning, James. I hope you were able to get some sleep on that lumpy bed last night."

"I slept great, thanks. I always thought our air back home was clean enough, but this morning air is really energizing. You guys live in the most amazing place I've ever been."

"Thanks, James. Truth is, we agree with you. Just don't tell everyone…if word gets out, this place will get just as crowded as everywhere else in the world." James looked to see if his aunt was kidding, but he couldn't tell. She was smiling, either at her own small observation or at the beauty of a crisp October morning.

"What would you like to eat, James?" Richard interrupted his thoughts. "We have fruit and cereal, or I could cook you a couple of eggs if you'd like."

He was cut short by the sound of a vehicle coming up the lane. Something was approaching that sounded like a World War I airplane running out of gas. As James watched, a red pickup truck crested the small hill and approached the house. At least, he thought it was red; most of it was rust-colored. He noticed the door on the passenger side was a dull blue metallic color, as if someone had run out of paint and decided it didn't matter too much. The bumpers and fenders were banged up in almost every possible spot. It was undoubtedly the most beat up vehicle James had ever seen that wasn't sitting in a junkyard.

"Hello, Corey," Uncle Richard hollered. "Didn't expect to see you out this early."

"Well, I forgot to water my watch last night, so it might be off a bit." The man named Corey shook his wristwatch next to his left ear, as if he expected it to catch up to the correct time by doing so. He was a stump of a man, not nearly as tall as Courtney and Richard, but what he lacked in height he made up for in width. *Maybe that's what they mean by barrel-shaped*, thought James. He wore faded blue overalls and had shocks of grey hair coming out in all directions from under an oily UK cap. James guessed that it might have been blue once, but he couldn't really tell.

"Why, hello, young man. Wait a minute..." Corey sniffed the

air like a hound dog who's run across a lost scent. "I believe I smell a cave explorer! Yes! Yes! You've got that Stephen Bishop dust all over you, son."

James was slightly taken aback by Corey's attention. Could he really smell the cave dust on him? And how did he know about James's adventures involving Stephen's treasure? He stood up uncertainly.

"James, just take everything Corey says, turn it upside down, and believe none of it, and you'll get it about right." Aunt Courtney grinned at their new guest; they were clearly old friends.

"Now them's hard words, ma'am, hard words. Here I come all this way to help out this old goat you call a husband, and you would have the young explorer to doubt me already."

James felt like he was half a step behind in this conversation, but he found himself smiling as the banter flew.

" I see your aunt doesn't see fit to introduce me, son. Corey Chaney at your service, last surviving veteran of the war between the states."

What?!? Just as he thought he was getting a handle on this scene being played out before him in the front porch, their guest had thrown him another curve. Hadn't the Civil War ended in the 1860's ??

"Oh, I know, most folks can't believe it. I don't look a day over ninety, do I?"

The old man was so animated and his eyes sparkled so dynamically when he talked that James had no idea what was real and what wasn't. *It couldn't be,* he reasoned. *It just doesn't add up...* He felt totally unprepared to speak, but it looked like the old man was waiting for him to say something.

"Uh, which side did you fight on, sir?"

"Well, both actually. You see, I joined the Confederate army when I turned seventeen, but it turned out fighting a war and watching men die in the mud wasn't as exciting as it was cracked up to be. Then I saw which way the wind was blowing, so I moved to Washington, DC, and became a Union man."

Corey was warming up to his tale, and his three listeners were getting drawn in. "In time I became part of the president's personal guard. You know, Abe and I used to play cards together. He used to let me come in the back door of the White House, on account of his wife Mary didn't care for me too much. Good woman, Mary, most of the time, but occasionally her cuckoo didn't come completely out of the clock door."

James couldn't help staring as Corey rambled. He looked at his aunt and uncle to see their reactions. They were both grinning with vast and tolerant amusement, as if they'd heard all this before but still found the old man entertaining.

"Yessir, I brought him some good ole Kentucky moonshine for his birthday that year. I think Mary must've poured it down the drain, though. Probably for the best...he had a lot on his mind." Corey peered under his bushy eyebrows directly at James. The boy remained silent.

This guy will say anything, James thought. *But he sure is a riot.*

"James, close your mouth." Richard chimed in. "You look like your jaw has come unhinged. Meet Corey Chaney, who never served anyone a day in his life, and who was born a good eighty years after the last battle was fought on this soil."

James looked back to Corey, who was still enjoying his own joke. "Pleased to meet you, sir."

Uncle Richard continued. "Corey's a local archaeologist and an expert on the native people of this area. He'll be along to help us today."

"And daylight's a-wasting, too," Corey chimed in." Let's head toward that big hole in the ground that everyone seems to be so taken with."

"We were just getting ready to feed James a little breakfast," Uncle Richard responded. "How about if you get some helmets ready and we meet you in about half an hour?"

"Half an hour! And I thought my grandmother was slow." The old man shook his head in disbelief as he climbed into his beat up truck. "I just hope the cave is still there when you get there."

Chuckling to himself, Corey fired up his trusty ride and bumped on over the hill.

"What's Corey helping with, Uncle Richard?"

"He and I will be leading two groups in the cave this morning. I intend to go explore Wright's Rotunda. I believe Corey wants to tackle Blackall Avenue. Both locations have some valuable American Indian artifacts; we may even find some new items today, you never know. You and Shanda would be welcome to join either group."

James had never been to either location, as far as he knew. The cave names sounded mysterious and exotic to him. He would sure be keeping an eye out; maybe he and Shanda could discover some more long-lost treasures in Mammoth Cave!

*****

Red and Rodney pulled on their green coveralls, in preparation for the day's caving activities. Although their clothes looked exactly like everyone else's, they had one key difference. The inside linings of their caving suits had special pockets sewn into them...pockets which nobody could see from the outside.

"Do we need the map, pardner?"

"No, we'd better leave it here. We don't want to arouse suspicion."

"OK. We know the passages by now, anyway. We'd better, after all the studying we've done."

Chapter IV

Uncle Richard and James met Shanda and her uncle at the equipment dormitory at nine o'clock. Corey came over to meet them and greet Matthew.

"Ranger Matthew, are you joining us this morning, or do you have some small children to lose in the cave today?"

James couldn't believe what he was hearing. Apparently, Corey enjoyed harassing everybody.

"Not today, thanks," Matthew replied. "I've got a troop of Cub Scouts to lead into the bottomless pit. Most of them usually make it out in a day or two."

Shanda cackled at her uncle's remark. *No need to worry here*, James realized. *Corey's friends can give it back as fast as they get it.*

James noticed his uncle chatting with a number of the visiting archaeologists; he was dying to talk to them, but he knew he'd have to wait. Maybe once they were in the cave he could find someone to talk to.

"Ladies and gentlemen, thank you all for making the effort to come to the park," Uncle Richard welcomed the group. "What we have planned for you should certainly make it worth your time. This morning, Corey Chaney and I will lead separate trips to the back of Main Cave, or Broadway, as it is called today. I know I don't have to remind any of you of the significance of these prehistoric artifacts, still lying where they were originally found. Feel free to take pictures, but under no circumstances are you to touch them or handle them in any way. Are there any questions before we head out?"

"Yes, " one man answered. "Remind us of what precautions we're taking to prevent WNS from spreading, please."

What on earth is WNS? James wondered. He looked at Shanda, but she just shrugged. *I'll ask Uncle Richard when I get a chance.*

His uncle was talking to the group about boots and coveralls and the importance of making sure that everything was decontaminated. He mentioned biosecurity mats at one point in his discussion, further piquing James's curiosity.

Decontamination? Biosecurity?? Sounds like terrorists have established a camp in the cave.

Corey noted his confusion. "Don't worry, James, we just get hosed down with sulfuric acid after the trip. People's eyes almost never get dissolved."

Uncle Richard ignored his friend as he answered James's questioning look. "WNS is white-nosed syndrome. We just clean our boots and clothes to be sure we don't carry disease spores in and out of the cave. It affects bats, but not people. We're just trying to be careful."

Soon they were walking down the hill toward the Historic Entrance. As the cool air rose to meet them, James felt the same thrill he experienced each time he approached the ancient cave. After he and Shanda had been banned from reentering last summer, he'd been dying to get back in. He could tell from his friend's upbeat mood that she was looking forward to their day's trip as much as he was. No one had suggested that they couldn't go, so their punishment must be over, he thought.

At the entrance, the visiting scientists divided into groups. James and Shanda wanted to stay together.

"Let's go with Corey," the boy suggested. "He's a great guy and I'll bet he knows a lot of cool stuff about the Indians."

As the two seventh graders joined the group forming around Corey, a friendly-looking lady approached. James thought she looked "outdoorsy." He wasn't exactly sure what that even meant, but he'd heard the word applied to a lot of people around the park. He figured it meant that someone would rather spend their time hiking outdoors than shopping in a mall.

"Hi, you two. I'm Carol; you must be James and Shanda. I heard about your big find last summer."

"Pleased to meet you, Carol." Shanda replied for both of them, while James nodded. "Are you a real archaeologist?"

"As real as it gets," Carol smiled. "I work for the Smithsonian in Washington. Early Woodland people are my specialty."

James chimed in. "Carol, I have a lot of questions about the Indians who used this cave. Could you talk to us, if you have time?"

Carol looked from James to Shanda, and back. "Of course. I love meeting kids who are interested in native culture, and naturally I love talking about my field. Let me tell you this, though, we hardly ever call these folks Indians any more. That's an old term. Did you know Columbus came up with it when he thought he'd landed in the Indies? Before he showed up, no one called them Indians."

"What tribes were they? Shawnee?"

"No, those tribes came much later. These people were their distant ancestors. They probably had names for their own people, but we have no way of knowing what they were. You know, there was no written language in the New World before Columbus came. Many cultures had symbols and hieroglyphics, but no one had developed a way to express thoughts using sentences and punctuation yet."

Shanda joined in. "Why do we call them natives, Carol? It looks to me like they just got here a little before the Spanish people. Aren't we all new to the New World?"

"That's a great question, Shanda, and a lot of folks think that's true. It's not at all, though. These people lived in this area for fourteen thousand years, at least. That's hundreds of generations. The first pioneers started entering Kentucky less than three hundred years ago. So we're definitely the newcomers here."

While they were talking, Corey had been arranging his fifteen visitors into pairs, with Carol left over.

"Good morning, professor," Carol spoke to him. "Looks like a fine day to go underground."

"Always a good day for that, friend. Carol, how would you feel about pairing up with James and Shanda today? They're pretty bright kids; I believe you might learn something from them if you pay attention."

"Only if you'll try to stay out of the way, you old slowpoke." She turned to the two friends. "Did you know that Corey was a friend of Geronimo? That is, until he asked if he could marry the chief's daughter. Then he had to hightail it out of there. He still limps a little from where he took an arrow in his rear end."

Corey smirked at her good-natured ribbing. *It looks like everyone here knows each other already*, James thought. *Maybe they have a big archaeologists club. I'll ask Carol; I sure would like to join that.*

Corey rounded up his group. "We'll head directly to Blackall Avenue, which should take about forty-five minutes or so. That section has more artifacts than you can shake a stick at. I'll show you some nice items, and then we'll hunt around a little."

*****

During the preparations, Red and Rodney made sure to get with Corey Chaney's group. The old professor wouldn't pay too much attention to them in the cave, and the rest of the group looked harmless enough. There was a married couple from

Ohio, assorted archaeologists from the eastern U.S., and the Smithsonian woman talking to a couple of kids. They put on their helmets and followed the group down the stairs into the cool darkness.

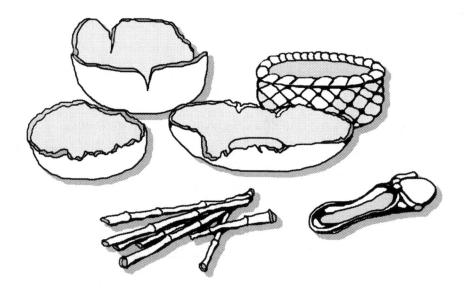

Chapter V

Entering the cave always had the same effect on James: it was magic. As Houchins Narrows opened into the Rotunda, he always felt life aboveground slip away. He was in the dark subterranean world again, with senses heightened to every sight and sound. The enormous, circular cave room was magnificent, and the last remnants of the surface breeze enchanted the travelers.

The group did not linger; some of them were new to Mammoth, but this was not a tour. As they hiked through briskly, James recognized Standing Rocks, the Giant's Coffin, and the Star Chamber as they passed. He had never been further than Star Chamber, and he was excited as Corey led them into new territory deeper in the cave. The older man was not as fit as he once was, but he could still move at a good clip on the trail.

Shanda picked up their conversation again. "What did these people eat, Carol? Corn and beans?"

"No, not at all. The earliest people in this cave were hunter-gatherers. Remember, they explored this place over four thousand years ago, beginning sometime before 2,000 B.C. Corn didn't make its appearance here as a reliable crop until sometime around 900 A.D. They did manage the land with fire, though."

Manage the land, thought James. *What were they doing, selling tickets?*

"By that I mean they were burning off large tracts to attract grazing animals like buffalo," the archaeologist continued. "Their earliest agricultural products were gourds, sunflowers, and chenopods. Those last plants are ancestors of today's lamb's quarters, a common weed. They harvested the seeds for grain."

"What were they doing in the cave, and why did they come so far into it?" James inquired. The two friends noticed that they had walked a good way into the cave without stopping. James guessed they had passed the one mile mark some time ago.

"Wow, you guys are asking great questions. The answer would take a long time to really explain, but basically they were removing minerals. Do you see that black crust on the walls?"

As the two seventh graders looked at the stone walls, they noticed that they were covered with a layer of blackened minerals. It looked like a thick, crunchy layer of soot.

"That's gypsum. And originally it was white and crystalline, but a couple thousand years of smoky torches and lanterns has blackened them completely. Now look; do you see that it's been removed as high up the wall as a person can reach? All the gypsum has been excavated from the cave walls for miles through these passages. We know that they were here, and we can see what they were doing, but it's only a guess as to what they did with all the minerals."

James was fascinated by this friendly woman and her knowledge of native people.

"Carol, how can I get to be an archaeologist some day?

"The first thing is, do the very best you can in school," she smiled. "That will open opportunities for you that you can't even dream about at your age. Our country and world need all the educated citizens we can get. I certainly hope both of you are planning on going to college. Later on, if you like archaeology, you can take college or university classes to learn more about it."

As they proceeded through some of the largest rooms in the cave, James and Shanda could not disguise their amazement. The first, Wright's Rotunda, was so huge that they couldn't see the whole room at once! The archaeologists stared in wonder as their beams played off the limestone walls.

"OK, enough lollygagging!" Corey moved them on.

After another brief walk, the group came to a halt, cutting off conversation. A new and unexpected noise greeted them: the sound of rushing water.

"We're at a spot where the cave roof leaks, producing this waterfall." Corey was walking down a pile of breakdown as he spoke. "You folks sit tight a minute; I'll light 'er up for you."

As he spoke, he descended into a pit at the base of the falls. "We call this the Cataracts!" he shouted over the noise of the cascade. Suddenly, he stuck his arm directly underneath the torrent and turned on his flashlight. The beam rode up the falling water column forty feet above his head! In the surrounding darkness, it was spectacular.

The group gasped and cheered as Corey scrambled back up the hill, soaked to his shoulder. "It doesn't get any better than that now, does it? Well come on, we're close to Blackall Avenue now."

About ten minutes later, they arrived at the base of their passage. It had taken almost an hour to walk the two-mile route, and the visitors were ready to get to the good stuff.

"What we'll find here," Corey was explaining, "will be cane reed torches used by the earliest people in the cave. If we're lucky, we may find some bone or shell scraping tools. Everything we encounter in this area carbon dates back between 0 and 1000 B.C. Remember, take all the pictures you want, but *don't* touch anything, please."

As they clambered up into the high-level passage, James felt a cool breeze caressing his face and shoulders. Almost immediately, Corey began to show his visitors piles of cane reed torches. The burnt sticks lay everywhere.

"Carol," Shanda asked in a quiet voice. "Were these really left here by ancient people?"

"Yes they were. I know how you feel; I felt the same way you do when I first came in here. It's hard to believe that they've been lying here all those thousands of years."

"Are there many arrows in here?" James asked.

"Actually, arrows weren't invented until a good deal later," Carol replied,

"These people used spears to hunt. And no, no one has ever found a weapon in the cave."

As the group walked slowly up Blackall Avenue, they shined their lights and excitedly shared their finds with their expedition mates.

"Here's some string. Looks like it might be made of vines twisted together."

"I think this might be a chipping tool. It's a flat rock with a sharpened edge."

"Corey, have you seen this pictograph? It looks like lightning bolts drawn on rock!"

The group was astounded at what they were witnessing. *What a treasure trove*, thought James. *Who knew this cave held so much ancient history? And I never would have guessed that Corey was such an expert.*

Indeed, Corey was enjoying showing off the cave's treasures and explaining them to the guest scientists. Shanda and James were absorbing every word he said.

At the end of the half-mile passage, Corey turned to face the group. "I know many of you want to take notes and pictures. Feel free to look around the passage, but remember, our mission here is to preserve and protect. Very few people ever see this passage. Please be careful not to move or damage anything."

*****

When Corey let the group wander, two men began to slowly search around the cave edges.

"Here's an old moccasin!" Red whispered. "Stand in front of me."

The two men had devised a method to hide their activity. By standing near the edge of a passage, one could block other people's view of his partner's actions.

As he spoke, Red pulled out a small plastic bag and dropped his find into the inner lining of his coveralls. "All clear."

They moved back and forth through the artifact trove, taking a few pictures to keep anyone from getting suspicious. When they got a chance, they teamed up to gather up the ancient items and hurriedly hide them in their coveralls. In a very short time, they had collected a number of tools, a small piece of cloth, pieces of two gourds, three moccasins, and a large number of prehistoric torch fragments.

"Red," the shorter man whispered. "I think those kids are looking at us!"

Fifty yards up the passage in the dim lantern light, Shanda was frantically tugging at Carol's sleeve.

"Just a minute, babe. Whatever it is, it's not going anywhere."

"Carol! I just saw that man pick up something and put it in his pocket!"

Carol straightened up quickly and stared down the passageway. "Oh, no. That's Dr. Sanders and his assistant. He's a famous archaeologist. I'm sure the shadows are just playing tricks on you."

"No they weren't, I promise!" Shanda was anxious for someone to believe her, but neither Carol nor James could confirm her suspicions. As she watched, the two men turned away from her and moved on up Blackall Avenue.

Chapter VI

Shanda's stomach was hurting, and she was beginning to sweat. She knew what she had seen, and she feared that once they left the cave, there would be no way to prove that the men were thieves.

"James!" She spoke in a quiet, urgent voice. "I can't let those two steal these treasures. I can't!"

"Let's stay with them as we exit the cave," her friend suggested. "If we see anything that looks suspicious, we can tell Uncle Richard. If they took anything, we can probably spot some lumps in their pockets."

"OK, help me keep an eye on them." Shanda wasn't totally satisfied, but she wasn't sure what she could do about the situation. If she charged a famous scientist with being a thief, she would probably be laughed at or worse. No one would believe a girl with no proof of her accusations.

As the group walked on toward the exit at Violet City, they met Uncle Richard's party. Like their own, the members of the troop were excited by their morning's discoveries. They each eagerly told of their special finds, constantly interrupting one another in their enthusiasm. James noticed that Shanda's suspect was notably uncommunicative. He and his assistant walked slightly behind the group, talking quietly. It looked to James like a perfect way to avoid talking to other group members.

Uncle Richard was thrilled at the morning's success. Each one of the archaeologists thanked him for allowing them access to the rare collection, made all the more special by being preserved inside the cave. He smiled as James came alongside.

"Uncle Richard, I know you don't want to hear this right now, but we've got a problem." Richard looked concerned, and James continued quickly. "Shanda saw two men putting artifacts in their pockets."

"What??! Was she sure about that? Everyone in this group is a nationally known scientist. I can't believe..."

"That's what Carol says, too. She can't believe anyone here would do that. But Shanda's positive that she saw Dr. Sanders pick up some items in the cave."

Uncle Richard looked around quickly, checking to see if anyone had heard his nephew. "James, please don't say anything to anyone about this. I'll do my best to keep an eye on them, but I can hardly believe that Red Sanders would take anything out of the cave."

As they walked up the stairs leading out of the cave, Richard hung back to talk with Dr. Red Sanders. "We're mighty pleased you gentlemen could join us for this conference," he spoke. "I hope you haven't been disappointed with our cave artifacts this morning."

James edged closer, trying to hear the conversation.

"No, quite the opposite," Dr. Sanders replied. "Rodney and I were just commenting on the wealth you have here. This has to be one of the top prehistoric collections in the country." *He sure sounds friendly enough,* James thought. *I wonder if Shanda really was tricked by the odd shadows in the cave.*

The group exited from the cavern into a large, wooded sinkhole. A green bus waited to take them back to their starting point at the visitors center. The archaeologists were still sharing notes on their morning's activities as they boarded.

"Folks, we'll do our best to stay on schedule with the research paper presentations this afternoon," Richard announced. "Please meet in the conference room by 1:45, so we can begin right at 2:00 o'clock."

Carol caught up with the two friends as they were getting off the bus. "I hope you two will join us for some of the presentations this afternoon and this evening," she said. "I can tell by your questions this morning that you would enjoy them."

James nodded eagerly, but as he looked at Shanda, he could see that she staring in the direction of Dr. Sanders.

"Look!" she whispered loudly. "Those two men have lumps under their coveralls! I knew it. I knew it!"

"Hang on there, Shanda," Carol urged. "That could be

anything. My clothes get bunched up under my coveralls all the time. Please don't accuse them of anything just yet."

"Are you suggesting we just let them steal those valuable artifacts?" James had never seen his friend this upset; she was practically trembling.

"No, not at all. But if we make them suspicious, they'll be doubly careful not to make any mistakes."

"Carol, can we ask the park rangers to search their rooms?" James asked.

"No, they would need a search warrant for that, James. It's against the law for the police to just search through your stuff anytime they feel like it. How would you like it if someone you didn't know could check your house whenever they felt like it? Even if you were totally innocent, you still wouldn't want to be treated that way."

James knew she was right, but there had to be an exception for criminals, didn't there?

"But what if we *know* they're hiding something valuable?"

"If a police officer can show enough evidence to convince a judge that he has a good reason to suspect someone, he may get a search warrant. Otherwise, the law says that we each get our privacy. It's in the Constitution, James."

The whole situation was very frustrating to him. If the rangers would just look in Dr. Sanders's room, they'd find all the proof they would need.

Carol urged her two young friends once again to join the afternoon conference session, then she and the others headed back to their motel rooms.

"James, you just gave me a great idea!" Shanda had been thinking while Carol had been telling them why the police couldn't help at this stage of the investigation. "Maybe the law can't look for evidence, but we can."

James wasn't sure he liked the sound of that. What did Shanda mean, anyway? He hurried to catch up with her.

"OK, we need to know which room they're in. You go around the far side of the building and up the stairs to the second floor. I'll walk through the first floor from this end. Maybe we can get lucky and see them going to their room. Hurry!"

Well, I guess there's nothing illegal about walking in a motel hallway, thought James. *Let's hope this doesn't get out of hand.*

He quickly ran around the end of the building and entered the door at the far end. Once inside, he was confronted with a flight of steps, just as Shanda had predicted. *Here goes nothing*, he thought to himself, and went up the stairs, taking them two at a time. As he rounded the corner onto the second floor, he saw several of the archaeologists just reaching their rooms. At the far end stood Dr. Sanders and his assistant!

James walked down the hall toward them. His heart was thumping so loudly in his chest that he was sure the two men would look his way. Right before they entered their room, he passed them and kept walking. They didn't appear to notice him at all, let alone the fact that he was about to have a nervous breakdown. As the door closed, James looked back to see the room number. It was 208.

Gotcha! he thought, then ran off down the stairs to meet Shanda.

Chapter VII

"James," Shanda spoke between bites of her BLT, "we've got to find a way to get into that room. If we can find any of those artifacts, then I'm going to tell the park rangers. We need *proof*, James."

"You've got that right. But Shanda, we got in trouble for sneaking into the cave last summer. Let's not do anything that's against the law; if we caught, I'll be grounded until I'm eighteen! And, you know, I really don't want to disappoint my parents again."

"I know what you mean, James. Don't forget though, we ended up heroes even though we got in trouble at the same time. We won't do anything crazy, but I just can't let them leave the park with those ancient relics."

The two teenagers were eating on the porch outside the coffee shop. The day was perfect, with a light breeze and a clear blue sky, but they hardly noticed that now. As they chatted, Corey Chaney ambled over with a plate of his own.

"Greetings, young cavers! How'd you like our trip this morning? Nothing works up an appetite like looking at some really old stuff in a big dark hole!"

James and Shanda appreciated Corey's friendliness, but the old man quickly noticed their blue mood. "What's got you two looking like hound dogs now? Wouldn't they serve you in the hotel bar?"

The kids smirked, in spite of themselves. "Corey, we've got a problem." It was James who spoke first. "Shanda saw two men stealing Indian artifacts from the cave, but we have no proof and no one will believe us."

Shanda gave James a grateful look; at least he believed her, which meant they were in this together. Corey's expression changed as quickly as a cloud coming over the sun. "Are you sure, young lady? I want to help you, but we need to be positive. Maybe they picked up some items to take pictures. They were expressly told not to do that, but there would be no crime involved. If they really removed things from the cave, then they are breaking federal law."

"Yes, sir, I'm as sure about this as I've ever been about anything. I saw those two men pick up some of the artifacts and hide them inside their coveralls. We want to look in their room, but Carol told us we need a search warrant."

Corey sat thoughtfully for a couple of minutes. "Well, the *police* are the ones who need a warrant," he said. "Normally I wouldn't dream of doing anything like this, but I'm forced to agree with you. I think we need to find a way to look in their room."

James and Shanda looked at each other with excitement. Corey was actually going to help them!

James piped up. "One time, when we were at a motel, my mom lost the card that opened the door. All she had to do was go to the desk and get another one."

"Not a bad idea, son. If only we knew which room they were staying in."

"It's room 208," Shanda jumped in excitedly. "James scoped it out for us. The man's name is Dr. Sanders."

"Red Sanders??! I can hardly believe that. Well, come to think of it, though, he did get into trouble at his old university job a few years back. I believe he was caught trying to sell some university property. After he was caught, he claimed that he was only getting rid of extra items no one needed, but I don't think many people believed him."

"I knew it!" said Shanda. "That man has 'low-down, sneaky thief' written all over him."

"OK. Tell you what we'll do. Once they're safely in their afternoon sessions, I'll get a key card for their room. I'd love to have your assistance, but I can't let you do that. It's too dangerous."

Shanda was glad for his help, but she wasn't going to hand over the whole excursion to the older man. "But we *want* to help, Corey. If nothing else, we can stand guard at the door."

"OK, you can do that much. We can post one of you on the stairs and the other one near the door. I don't particularly want to get caught looking through someone else's belongings."

"Thank you, Corey. I was afraid they were going to get away

with it. Now I just know that we'll get to the bottom of this." Shanda was excited, and James could feel his pulse start to race. He sure wanted to be in on the action, too.

At 1:45, James and Shanda were sitting outside the door of the hotel conference room. Uncle Richard had spent his lunch hour making final preparations, making sure his projectors and microphones worked. Now satisfied that everything was ready for the afternoon sessions, he stepped outside to catch some air before the program began.

"Hi guys, good to see you here. Have you decided which talks you are going to attend?"

"We've been looking it over," James replied. "Honestly, there's nothing in this first hour that we're interested in. Carol's talk at 3:00 looks good, though. We'll be around for that one."

"Suit yourself. Dr. Logan's talk at 2:00 on ancient DNA may be a little technical for you, but I still think you'd enjoy hearing about his research."

As 2:00 approached, the visiting scientists arrived singly or in small groups for the afternoon sessions. As James and Shanda saw Dr. Red Sanders and his assistant approach the room, they stepped out into the hall, where Corey could see them. The older man was sitting down in the hotel lobby, outside the gift shops. Sticking with their plan, Shanda gave Corey a casual wave. As she did, James climbed the motel stairs up to the second floor. Once again, his heart was pounding, but nothing like it had that morning. *Maybe I'm getting the hang of this detective work*, he thought to himself.

James positioned himself at the top of the stairs, where he could see the stairwell below him, as well as the second floor hallway. As he watched, Corey and Shanda came up the stairs at the other end of the hall and casually approached room 208. Even from this distance, James could see that Shanda was excited. Everything about her body language screamed "Let's go!", but Corey shuffled along at his normal speed. No one would ever know that he was doing anything but walking and talking with his young friend.

As they approached the locked door, Corey pulled a plastic key card from his pocket. James's plan had worked. Now all they had to do was find the stolen loot!

Corey casually opened the door and stepped inside. He didn't want to leave it open any longer than he needed to. Turning toward Shanda, he was about to tell her to keep an eye on things in the hall, when she slipped past him into the room.

"Shanda! What are you doing?" Corey was agitated, but he spoke in a loud whisper. "You can't come in here! Stay outside and do your job, like we agreed."

Shanda was already heading toward the closet. "Change of plans, sir. I can't let you have all the fun. Besides, we can get out of here that much faster if we both look."

Corey didn't want to waste time arguing with the girl, so he quietly closed the door and followed her into the room.

James was confused. The last he'd heard, Corey was going to do a quick search of the room while Shanda waited outside. Now, if anyone came up the other staircase, no one would be at the door to warn them. *Time to move*, he thought, and jogged quickly down the hall toward room 208.

He tapped on the door. "Shanda!" he whispered. "What are you doing in there?"

Receiving no answer, he turned the door handle. It opened! James looked up and down the hall, but saw no one in either direction. He opened the door just a bit and slipped inside.

"James, what are you doing here?" Corey exclaimed. He was clearly upset. "You're supposed to be keeping watch."

As he spoke, Shanda's voice came from the closet. "James, come here, quick. I found their coveralls. This closet is too small for me and Corey, but you might fit in here."

"You two are going to ruin everything!" Corey hissed. "Be quick. I'll keep watch in the hall." The two friends heard the door open behind them, and Corey was gone.

"OK, James. You check this one and I'll take the other." She handed him a large dirty pair of coveralls. They looked exactly like the ones the scientists had worn just a few hours earlier. "This is exciting, isn't it!"

As nervous as they both were, James and Shanda were thrilled to be taking part in this adventure together. They knew they could get in trouble for being where they didn't belong, but they both thought that, if they found the stolen artifacts, their transgression would be forgiven.

"Shanda." James spoke. "These coveralls have big pockets sewn on the inside, but they're empty!"

"Same here." As they spoke, the two kids didn't hear the

quiet insistent rapping at the door. "Here's a suitcase." Shanda continued. let's see if they've stashed the items in here."

As she approached the closed suitcase on the bed nearest the window, they heard the lock click and saw the door start to open.

"Everything OK, Corey?" James whispered.

"Hey!" an angry voice shouted. "What the heck are you doing in my room?"

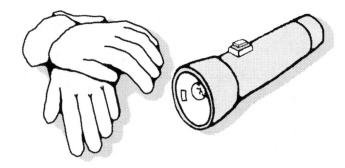

Chapter VIII

James's head started to spin. His thoughts got very confused very quickly, as if he'd dropped his brain in a blender. He felt weak and could barely focus, let alone talk to the man who addressed him. He was afraid he would pee his pants if he didn't pull himself together, fast.

Red Sanders was furious. "I'm not going to ask you again, son. If you don't answer me, we'll go find some park police to chat with!" He grabbed James roughly by the shoulder, pinning him to the wall near the door.

"I'm…I'm sorry, sir," James stammered. As he spoke, he realized that Red was in trouble himself. He obviously couldn't tell the park police anything. If they searched the room, the police would find his stolen goods. That didn't rule out the possibility that he might decide to rough up James a little, but even as mad as he was, he didn't look ready to strike. It gave him a bit of courage.

"My uncle is Ranger Richard, who is in charge of the

conference. He asked me to get some papers from one of the speakers' rooms. I was sure he said room 208, but it might have been 206."

"How did you get in here?" Sanders asked roughly. "Who gave you a key?"

"The cleaning lady was out on the landing, and I asked her if she could let me in for just a second," James lied. If he could stop his heart from exploding out of his chest, he just might get out of here alive and unhurt.

As if sent by an angel, there was a knock on the door.

"Housekeeping!" a woman's voice called. As she spoke, they could hear the sound of her key card entering the slot on the door.

Red Sanders looked skeptical, annoyed, and confused all at once. He wanted to believe that no one had found his stash of stolen goods, and James's story sounded as if it might actually be true. No harm, no foul. He released the boy's arm from his strong grip as he spoke to the maid entering the room

"We don't need housekeeping service today. Thank you, ma'am." The small woman backed out and was on her way. Red stood about two feet away from James, mulling over his predicament.

"Dr. Sanders. I am *really* sorry I came into your room by mistake. I would never come into someone's private room without permission." James could see that the crisis was over, and amazingly he had the good sense to stop talking. He didn't want to sound as desperate as he felt.

The man seemed to sense there was no advantage in making

a big deal out of the situation. If anyone checked his room, it wouldn't go well with him. "OK, son, maybe I was a little hasty. But I've got to admit, I was shocked to find you in here. How did you know my name, anyway?"

"We were in the same group in the cave this morning. My uncle and Corey were telling me about what a famous archaeologist you are."

"Alright, I've got to get back to the conference sessions. From now on, if you need to go into someone's room, you need to ask them first. Is that clear?"

"Yes, sir. Very clear." James was breathing easier already. It looked as if this crisis had been averted, and he and Shanda could...

Shanda! He had totally forgotten about her! He hadn't heard a peep since Red Sanders had caught him; he was pretty sure the scientist didn't suspect that he had an accomplice.

As the scientist shooed James toward the door, he seemed to stop and realize something. He quickly walked to the closet and threw open the door! The two pairs of coveralls hung where he had left them, alone in the closet. *Nice work, Houdini*, James thought to himself. Dr. Sanders then dropped to his knees and quickly looked under the bed. He grunted a little from the exertion of standing up, but he seemed to feel that everything was in order.

Under the bed! James thought excitedly. He desperately wanted a chance to take a look down there, but even as the thought was forming in his brain, he was being escorted from the room, one large hand on his shoulder.

Out in the hall, James saw no one. Corey and the cleaning

lady had both disappeared. There was no way he could hang around and wait for Shanda; he had dodged one bad situation, and he sure didn't need to get himself into another one. Dr. Sanders made sure the door was closed securely, then he headed toward the steps at the end of the landing. James walked slowly down the hall in the opposite direction. All he could do now was wait until Shanda reappeared.

As he walked across the bridge toward the visitor center, James stopped to relax and catch his breath. He knew he'd almost been caught doing something wrong, possibly even criminal. He knew, too, that his parents wouldn't understand his actions. He had promised them that he would behave responsibly, and he had just been caught sneaking into a hotel room illegally.

Looking around, he noticed the fall colors close to him on both sides of the foot bridge. Since he was thirty feet or so off the ground, he was even with the canopies of some large trees. Birds fed on the berries hanging under the red leaves of the poison ivy vines. He leaned on the railing and tried to relax. Below him, a group of visitors were walking down the hill, carrying lanterns. The Violet City Tour, headed toward the very artifacts he and Shanda had seen that morning. A large guide with a long, bushy beard led the group down the hill.

The boy cut back to the Troglobites Snack Bar for an ice cream. He had eaten lunch almost three hours earlier and his adventures had made him hungry. Besides, all he could do right now was wait.

"James!" Apparently, waiting time was over. Shanda approached him in a near run; he could tell she was excited.

"I found it, James! I found their stash under the bed!" Her eyes were on fire. "There's a large duffel bag under there. After you left, I pulled it out and bingo, it's loaded with artifacts. They got a *lot* of stuff out of the cave, James."

"Shanda, I was really worried about you. When Sanders opened the closet, I almost got sick. I thought for sure you were a goner."

"Nope. As soon as he pushed you up against the wall, I knew I had to get out of there. I dropped to the floor and scooted under the bed while he was shouting at you."

"Jeez, I've never been so scared in my life! When he grabbed me, I thought I was going to mess my pants!"

"You did great, James. Anyone would have been scared in that situation. That was quick thinking with the story about looking for something in the wrong room."

"Shanda, I have a terrible feeling about this whole thing. When I thought he was going to turn me in, my whole stomach was tied up in a knot. I thought I was going to be sick right there."

"That gave me a fright, too. Although you've got to admit, it sure was exciting, wasn't it? I'll bet you and I could open the Shanda and James detective agency." She giggled as she spoke. *This girl has nerves of steel*, thought James. But Shanda's relaxed attitude helped him, too. He was beginning to look at their afternoon's escapades as another exciting adventure with his friend from Tennessee.

Shanda went to the counter and bought an ice cream cone, while James enjoyed the October day. When she returned, he posed a question. "One thing that I've been wondering, Shanda. When Sanders looked under the bed, why didn't he see you?"

"I guess that was just my good luck. The duffel bag is pretty big, and I was lying on the other side of it from where he was crouching. After he left, I dragged it out and looked inside. James, it's packed with torches and tools; they even found an ancient moccasin. We are not going to let them get away with this!" Shanda was getting more and more excited as she talked. *I'm glad she's not mad at me*, James reflected. *I wouldn't want to be on her wrong side.*

After a few minutes, Shanda wound down and concentrated on eating her ice cream. "OK, James," she spoke more evenly now. "We need a plan, and it's got to be good."

"Shanda," James spoke, "I think I know just what to do next."

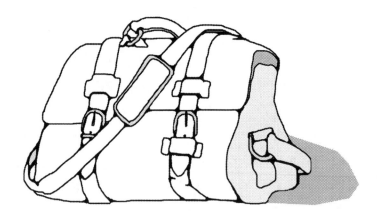

Chapter IX

The two young teenagers were in a pickle. They had the evidence they needed, but they couldn't very well admit to the park rangers that they had broken into a motel room to find it. They also knew that it was time to get some adults involved; they were in no position to confront the two thieves by themselves.

"How about if we just steal them back?" Shanda suggested. "We could…"

"Shanda! What are you talking about?? I'm usually the one with the harebrained ideas. I'm counting on you to be the sensible one here."

"Hah!" Shanna chortled. "OK, here I am, Miss Sensible! Seriously, James, Corey still has his key. If we sneak into the room one more time, we could get out with the duffel bag and they'd never even know it. I know what! We can dump the artifacts and stuff their bag back with newspapers! They won't notice the switch until they look in their bag, and that could be days!"

"But what would we do with the loot?" James didn't really like the sound of this plan, but he was curious.

"Put it back in the cave. I'll bet you anything Corey will help us. He's as mad about all this as we are. Once we get the artifacts out of their room, all we have to do is take them back to Blackall Avenue and be done with them."

James was not convinced. "I don't know. It sounds good, and it really might work. I'm just not crazy about doing anything illegal right now, especially after getting caught the first time. What really bugs me is that Sanders and his accomplice would get away with no penalties. They might even try again some day."

"I know, that's a problem for me too. Maybe I could just put some stink bombs on their car engine. Once it heats up on the drive home…" She grinned at the thought of all that nasty, smelly smoke working its way into the car.

James laughed out loud. After all the stress of the day, it was good to be able to joke around with his friend.

"Shanda, I say we find Corey and see what he says. He's already involved, and maybe he'll know what to do next."

"That sounds about right. I'd love to fix those two myself, but we need more than just you and me. Let's walk over to the conference and see if he's in one of the sessions."

When the two friends arrived at the Rotunda Room, they could see that the visiting scientists were standing in the hall, chatting. Their friend Carol came over to speak to them.

"Hi you two. I was hoping you might join us for a session

The Stolen Treasure of Mammoth Cave

or two. We have a ten minute break right now, then it's time for the second round. I wish you could have heard Dr. Logan's talk. That man has done wonders with his ancient DNA studies. Today he was telling us about ancient seeds that he's tested. His results indicate that people in this area may have been trading further afield a lot earlier than we thought."

James's curiosity was piqued. He temporarily forgot about their problem. "What kind of seeds did he study, Carol?"

"There's a wild plant called *Chenopodium*, or lamb's quarters. The Native Americans in this area actually cultivated it for grain. We have seeds from right here in Mammoth Cave which are almost four thousand years old."

"How does DNA tell you where they came from?" Shanda inquired.

"The DNA from these seeds matches that from plants in the eastern U.S. That means that these people traded with populations east of here a lot earlier than we originally thought. There are other types of *Chenopodium* in Mexico, but these plants don't match those. That's what I love about archaeology. Every new finding adds a little bit to our big picture of how these people lived." Carol smiled at her two new friends.

"Carol, thanks for sharing that," said Shanda. "Right now, we're looking for Corey. Have you seen him?"

"Yes, he was here just a second ago. He may be helping set up a screen in the second conference room, down the hall."

"Thanks, Carol. See you soon."

A few seconds later James and Shanda spotted the older man coming out of the room where Carol had seen him. He was moving at his usual leisurely pace; if the afternoon's activities had rattled him, it didn't show.

"Hello young cavers. Coming on our trip to connect to Fisher Ridge this evening?" By now they knew not to take Corey too seriously. James had heard that Fisher Ridge held the seventh longest cave in the world and that explorers had been trying to connect it to Mammoth for years. Corey had about as much chance of connecting the two caves as he had of hopping through the cave on a pogo stick.

"Corey, can we talk for a minute? Shanda found something today you might want to hear about."

The old man raised one hairy eyebrow. "Sure, let's take a stroll. I think they can muddle through the next session without my help."

Once they were outside the building and out of range of prying ears, the two adventurers told Corey about their experiences from the time he had left them, starting with James getting caught and finishing with Shanda's big news about finding the stolen treasures.

"Dr. Sanders was furious. Just thinking about it now makes me scared all over again."

"Don't worry, James. You guys did great, and there's nothing the good doctor can do to you now. Shanda, that's a great find you made. Now that we have proof, we have to figure out what to do with it."

"I wish we could call the park rangers and get them arrested," Shanda said earnestly, "but James doesn't think they can use the evidence because we broke into their room."

"Well, James is right about that," Corey mused. "We'll have to come at this from a different direction, is all."

"But the conference is over tomorrow morning." Shanda was still worried. She didn't want to get this close and let the two thieves get away.

"Corey," she continued. "Any chance we could go back into room 208 and steal the artifacts back? We could help you put them back in the cave, and no one would ever know they were gone."

"That's not a bad idea, Shanda. I think what we really need is to prove that these two men are guilty, so they can never do anything like this again."

The trio walked along a path away from the hotel, toward a locomotive sitting on the lawn. "Why is there a train on the grass out here?" James wondered aloud.

"That's old Engine # 4. Trains were used by park visitors to get here in the late 1800's and early 1900's, before cars became common. Several years ago this engine was cleaned up and put on display out here. In fact, the old track has been converted to a bike trail down to Park City."

Corey sure knows a lot about this place, James thought. *I wonder how long he's worked here.* As he daydreamed about Corey and Shanda worried about the artifacts, the older man was scanning the area near the camp store parking lot.

"Well, looky here," Corey suddenly cheered up. "Just who we were hoping to see on a fine fall day."

As the two kids looked up, a ranger patrol car pulled into the parking lot. A large, muscular man emerged from the police car, looking impressive in his uniform. *I wouldn't want to mess with him,* James thought. *He'd probably pull that gun on me for littering.*

"Hello there, crime dog!" Corey shouted across the lot. "Arrested any old ladies for walking their poodles too fast today?"

James was horrified at his friend's disrespect toward the officer, but he needn't have worried. "Why Corey Chaney, I thought we'd moved the homeless shelter out of the park. Is someone giving out free pork rinds today?"

The two men laughed, glad to see one another. The policeman turned toward the two seventh graders, his eyebrows riding up on his face. "Well, if it ain't the two top sleuths at Mammoth Cave. You two don't know me, but I saw you after all that hoo-haw you caused last summer. That was a nice piece of work, by the way. Jason Dowell, at your service."

The officer smiled as he spoke. Mr. Dowell reminded James of Mr. Curtis, one of his teachers back in Ohio. *I guess large strong guys can afford to be friendly,* he thought. *No one's going to mess with them anyway.*

Corey spoke up as Shanda and James shook the ranger's outstretched hand.

"I guess you're looking for that bag of glazed doughnuts someone reported missing. Try the second shelf down in the camp store. I hear the thief squirreled away some RC's in there, too."

"Thanks for the tip, old man. I don't know if I could get anything done around here without your good advice."

While they were chatting, Shanda had made a decision. "Mr. Dowell," she sounded earnest, and a little nervous, "There's something going on that you need to know about."

"You feel free to call me Jason, young lady. Now please, tell me what's on your mind." And Shanda spilled the beans.

Chapter X

Officer Dowell listened carefully as Shanda recounted everything that had happened, starting with the morning field trip. She explained what she had seen and how they had decided to investigate for themselves, a decision which had led them to their discovery of the stolen artifacts in room 208. The only thing she didn't mention was Corey's role in getting a room key; she didn't want to get him in trouble. Jason Dowell became more interested as her story developed, and when he finally understood the importance of what she was telling him, his genial smile was long gone.

"You have done the right thing coming to me, Shanda. You and James have done a nice piece of detective work, but this situation calls for our intervention. I won't bother to ask how you two managed to get into Red Sanders's room in the first place." He glanced in Corey's direction as he spoke, making sure the older man caught his meaning.

"They probably forgot to shut the door," Corey guessed. "You know how absent-minded those scientists can be."

"Sure, that's probably it." Jason replied. "Our real concern here is to recover the stolen goods. That part's easy; I could just go into their room and take them back. But what I really want to do is nail these two creeps so they won't sneak off with no punishment."

"I might have an idea," said James. "See what you think of this."

James spent the next several minutes explaining his scheme. The foursome kicked his ideas around a little and finally settled on a course of action they all liked. It would take some skilled acting and perfect timing, but they all agreed it was a possible way to trap the two thieves.

The midafternoon sun was already moving toward the western horizon. Now that their plan was in place, the two friends could only wait. After parting ways with Corey and Jason Dowell, they headed back toward the hotel conference room.

"James, I'm so nervous I feel like I might pass out," Shanda worried.

"I know what you mean, but all we can do now is let it all play out."

"What if it doesn't work? What if we don't catch them? What if they get away with it??" Shanda was getting worked up again. James was beginning to realize what a toll this whole episode was taking on his friend's nerves.

"No, don't worry, they won't get away with anything. With

Ranger Dowell and Corey on our side, we'll get the stolen artifacts back. I'm sure of that. The only thing we don't know is if we can catch Dr. Sanders and his sidekick while we're at it."

"Well, I'm not letting *them* go, that's for sure. I'll tackle them in the parking lot if I have to."

They talked until they had covered all the ground again. They were spent. James couldn't believe that just this morning they had taken the trip into the cave. It seemed like a week ago already.

The two allies arrived at the hotel as the conference was letting out for the afternoon. They hadn't attended any of the sessions. James was sad about that, but he knew they had done the right thing in taking the time to deal with the two criminals. *I just hope this plan works!* he thought for the twentieth time that afternoon.

"Hey you two. How's everything going?" They were greeted by Uncle Richard's voice right outside the hotel.

"Great, sir. How's everything with the conference?" James marveled at how calm Shanda sounded under the circumstances. They had agreed not to share their information with anyone else, including his aunt and uncle. James didn't feel great about that; it felt like he was lying by not revealing the truth. But Ranger Dowell had emphasized the importance of secrecy. James remembered his words "We don't want to give anything away that might hurt our operation."

Operation, he thought, *that's exactly what it is.*

"Shanda, our operation needs a name. What do you think? Operation Sneaky? Operation Trappers?"

"No, James, we're getting ready to nail these guys. We need something like Operation Rattlesnake or Black Widow. We are the predators and they are the prey."

"Yeah, good thought. Let's go with Operation Rattlesnake!"

So now, meeting up with Richard, they had to keep Operation Rattlesnake and everything about it under their hats. Not a word to anyone.

"How's everything going for you, Uncle Richard?" James inquired. "Are you about to wrap up the conference?"

"We're getting close. Today's sessions were excellent. I'm so glad that we were able to sponsor this event. We have our final dinner and guest speaker tonight. Everyone will head home early tomorrow."

"Can we come to the dinner?" Shanda asked.

"Of course, we wouldn't have it without you," Richard smiled. "I've got seats for you reserved at a table with Aunt Courtney and Carol, the archaeologist you met this morning. Shanda, I've asked your uncle to join us, but I haven't heard back from him yet."

"I'll make sure he comes, don't worry," the girl replied.

"Let me know if he can't; I'll ask Courtney to pick you up on the way."

"Thanks. I'll see if I can find him right now."

James and his uncle headed home to unwind, as Richard put it. It had been a big day for both of them. They had a few hours to relax before cleaning up for dinner. James texted his mom and dad, telling them what a great time he was having. Richard and Courtney retired to the back deck to chat and watch the sunset. As James approached them, he heard them laughing as his aunt recounted an incident from one of her cave tours.

"...so I tell them the entire story of Lost John as we're standing at Mummy Ledge. I showed them the cable and the boulder where he was trapped over two thousand years ago, and told how he was extracted from that spot in 1935. And then she asked 'and he was still alive??' Poor thing; the entire group did their best not to laugh out loud." They chuckled as they remembered other incidents and odd things they'd heard visitors say.

"I had a gentleman two days ago who insisted the cave ran underneath his property in Louisville. I tactfully tried to tell him that was impossible, but his mind was made up."

Sitting on the porch, James was able to forget his present worries for a few minutes. The trio watched the sun fall behind the ridge as the cool evening air worked it's way down the valley. A barred owl hooted its deep *who-cooks-for-you* up in the woods.

Aunt Courtney broke the evening reverie. "OK, guys, we need to leave in fifteen minutes or so. James, do you have some clean clothes you can put on for supper?"

Dinner in the hotel meeting room was excellent, and James and Shanda loved every minute. Uncle Matthew had accompanied Shanda to the program; they shared a table with James and Aunt Courtney, Carol, and three other conference participants. The two kids peppered Carol with all the questions which came into their heads, until Aunt Courtney called them off.

"Guys, let's give Carol a chance to catch her breath and maybe eat some supper. She might want to enjoy this fine meal we're having."

"Oh, no, that's completely OK." Carol spoke quickly. "I love talking to these two. Their questions are great, and it's a thrill for me to able to share my passion with them."

If Aunt Courtney were my mom, I could stick my tongue out at her right now, James reflected. *Probably shouldn't do it here, though.*

His aunt gave in. "Well, all right. But please be sure to tell them when you've had enough."

As dinner wound down, there was sound from the front of the room. "Folks, it's time for a few words from this evening's keynote speaker." Uncle Richard stood at the podium; James thought he looked cool.

"Our guest this evening is a gentleman that many of you know already. If you don't know him personally, you may have met him today, and I'm certain that you've read his research on archaic artifacts in North American caves. Please welcome the Kentucky state archaeologist and retired University of Kentucky professor, Dr. Corey Chambers."

What?! Doctor Corey Chambers?? James couldn't make sense of what he had just heard. Corey was no doctor; he was a crafty old man who loved the cave and everything in it. *State archaeologist??*

"Whoa," Shanda spoke into his ear, as the group gave Corey

a warm round of applause. "Your uncle just rearranged my position on good old Corey!"

"That's exactly what I was thinking. I had no idea..."

Corey's voice at the microphone cut him off. "Good evening, friends old and new. I am holding here a cane reed torch, with Richard's permission I might add. I hold this tonight to emphasize that this is not a prop put in the cave to show visitors. This piece of plant material is one of the keys to understanding who came to this spot before us. How did these native people live? What did they eat? Why did they come in the cave? What type of tools did they use?"

The audience was entranced. Corey was a gifted speaker whose mere presence commanded their interest.

"Archaeology is a wonderful science," he continued. "I like to think of it as solving a picture puzzle without most of the pieces or any idea of what the final image should look like. Honestly, I can't think of anything I'd rather be doing than studying the artifacts of those who came before us." Heads nodded; listeners smiled.

"Technology continues to provide us with new tools to study ancient objects. Recent studies in ancient DNA analysis have revealed exciting new information on the earliest days of native trading and agriculture in North America."

Corey talked for forty-five minutes about the American Indian artifacts which were his specialty. James and Shanda were riveted to every word; in fact, every eye in the room focused on Corey Chaney the entire time. His listeners knew they were in the presence of greatness. As he concluded and thanked the group, a vigorous applause started. Soon the group rose to their feet, clapping in salute to the famous man.

"Can't always judge a book by its cover, can you now?" Courtney laughed spontaneously.

"Aunt Courtney, why didn't you tell us? I thought Corey was an old guide who came by to help Richard with the conference!"

Shanda was just as excited as James. As the meeting broke up, Corey and Richard came over to their table, chatting at the success of the evening.

"Corey, that was amazing!" James burst out.

"Why, thank you son. I tried not to drool too much. And these Depends undergarments really come in handy when you're in the spotlight. Of course, it's like I told General Eisenhower at Normandy, sometimes they ain't quite enough."

James was confused momentarily, but when he saw Shanda and his aunt laughing their heads off, he got the picture. It was just Corey being Corey.

"Well, I'll see you two young 'uns in the morning. Richard and Matthew, any chance we could get these two over here by seven? I know they'll want to say goodbye to a couple of their new friends. Night all." And with that, the state archaeologist shuffled out into the evening.

Uncle Richard looked mildly confused. "What was that all about?" he asked.

"We've met some folks who are leaving early, and we wanted to say goodbye," James explained.

"Well, as they say in Louisiana, it's OK by me if it's OK bayou." Ranger Matthew nodded his approval as he grinned.

James and Shanda looked at each other in apprehension. During their meal and Corey's speech, they had completely forgotten about their secret plan. But tomorrow, it was show time!

Chapter XI

James didn't sleep much that night. He woke up at least once an hour, dozing fitfully in between. When the clock on the bed stand read 6:00 and the first light was turning the sky from black to gray, he hopped up and headed to the bathroom. Washing his face and dragging a brush through his hair, he was ready to roll five minutes later. The night before, he had talked to his aunt and uncle about getting to the park early. Courtney and Richard seemed curious, but they were early risers and didn't seem to mind the quick start. If Corey wanted them there at 7:00, they'd be there.

Uncle Richard hadn't spoken about the missing artifacts since the day before. James couldn't believe that he had forgotten about them completely, although Richard had been super busy coordinating the whole conference. Maybe he thought that Shanda had changed her mind about what she had witnessed. In any case, he didn't bring it up and James didn't want to rock the boat. The fewer people who knew abut their plan, the better.

James and his uncle arrived at the Mammoth Cave Hotel at 6:45. Very few people were stirring at this hour, although James noted a park patrol car parked near the lone road leading out of the lot. In the early morning light he couldn't see if anyone was inside the vehicle.

Shanda and Uncle Matthew arrived minutes later, and Corey came out from his room to meet them. The friends said their good mornings all around, and the park rangers left their young charges with Corey.

"Beautiful morning." The archaeologist looked around as he spoke. "Did you two get a good rest last night?"

"No," both kids answered in unison.

"I must have woken up twenty times." Shanda spoke. "Every time I rolled over I checked the clock."

"Me too," James added. "That was the longest night of my life."

"Well, I don't believe we'll have to wait too long this morning. I'm sure our two guests will want to make a quick exit. Officer Dowell checked their registration for us; they're driving a blue Honda. It's in the lot, not far from one of the end doors to the building."

"Let's go," said Shanda. "I'll be more comfortable when I know I'm actually doing something."

"I agree," Corey added. "Your two cell phones charged? We're only going to get one chance at this."

"Please, we're already scared enough!" James said. "Don't make it any worse."

"Actually, I'm not scared at all." Shanda smiled mischievously as she spoke. "I'm looking forward to busting those two punks."

"Corey, what if something goes wrong and we don't catch them?"

"Don't worry, James, they'll never get out of the parking lot. The park rangers are federal police; busting these two men will be about as hard as eating lunch for them. OK, you both ready?"

The two friends nodded their assent, and they headed out.

As Corey had predicted, they didn't have long to wait. About ten minutes later, Dr. Red Sanders and his accomplice came out of the door at the end of the building. Each was rolling a suitcase; in addition Rodney had two rumpled sets of coveralls bunched over his left arm. Sanders was carrying a large army-green duffel bag!

James felt his heart rate jump to about two hundred beats per minute as he watched them through he glass doors of the hotel lobby. In spite of his excitement, he felt controlled, and thrilled to be getting the operation underway. He watched carefully, as the two men threw the suitcases, dirty clothes, and duffel bag into the car trunk. Pushing the speed dial on his cell phone, he completed a three-way conference call with Corey and Shanda. James had hoped the park rangers would want to take part in his alert, but apparently they had their own ways of communication worked out already.

"Operation Rattlesnake, go! Go now!"

As he spoke, his two partners moved. Corey ambled up to the two scientists, looking like he didn't have a care in the world. "Good morning, gentlemen. Are you going to join us for our final breakfast before you go? The hotel restaurant puts out a nice buffet."

"Good morning, Dr. Chaney," Sanders replied. "We certainly enjoyed your talk yesterday evening. Rod and I were saying that it was a high point for both of us. This weekend has been a real boost for our professional careers. We'd love to join you, but we've got a lot of miles to put on the car today, so we need to head out."

Boy, you are one cool customer, thought James. *If I were you, I'd be sweating so much I'd need a raincoat.*

"Very understandable, son," Corey replied. "Not everyone can be fortunate enough to live in Kentucky." He gave the men an easy smile as he spoke. "Could you do me a quick favor before you head out? I'm supposed to collect contact information from everyone attending the conference, so we can all stay in touch about our research. It won't take a minute."

"No problem. Do you have something to write with?"

"I do right here in the lobby. Step in here for one minute, and we'll get you on your way. You sure you won't have a few biscuits and gravy?"

"I'd love to, but we'll have to pass."

Boy, Corey's a master at this. He's got these two eating out of his hand. As James saw the three men start to walk toward the hotel lobby, he ran down the hall and out the door on the end of the building.

As James moved to his new position, Shanda walked quickly out from behind a large cedar tree where she'd been waiting. Hoping that Red Sanders hadn't locked his car, she ran to the door and pulled. It opened! Corey had distracted the two men just at the right moment, drawing them away from their Honda. Shanda reached under the dashboard and popped the lever which opened the trunk. As James approached the car at a run, Shanda looked quickly at the bags in the trunk, then hopped inside! Her friend reached the back of the car just as she was settling in, and being careful not to knock her in the head, he slammed the trunk shut.

To James, the noise sounded deafening. He turned as casually as he could and scouted the parking lot. Corey and the two scientists were nowhere to be seen. He presumed they must still be inside the hotel lobby. Despite the noise of the slamming trunk, no one seemed to have noticed him or Shanda. The whole operation had taken ten seconds, tops. With his role done, the boy ran back toward the door at the end of the hotel, out of sight from the lobby area.

James stopped and peered through a large bush at the corner of the building. Moments later, Corey came out of the building with Dr. Sanders and Rodney, his assistant. The two scientists paid no attention to a park ranger, chatting with a friend right outside the building. The three men said their goodbyes, and Corey walked a little faster than usual back into the hotel.

James held his breath as they started the Honda and slowly

started moving. Shanda was in there! He had come up with this hair-brained scheme, and she had willingly agreed, but now he was really concerned that something might happen to her. But, just as the car started rolling, Shanda started screaming. Loud. So loud, in fact, that James could hear her from the end of the hotel building, and loud enough that Ranger Dowell could hear her clearly from his post near the door.

"Help! HELP!! They're kidnapping me! HEELLLPPP!" For just a minute, James thought she may have been overdoing it a bit; but really, if he were getting kidnapped, he'd scream like a banshee too.

At first, when Shanda's racket started, the two men inside the car didn't hear her. They looked up to see a law enforcement officer jogging toward them, one hand telling them to stop and the other circling over his head. As they watched in confusion, a park police car parked at the far end of the lot drove right at them with its red lights flashing.

"Gentlemen, please step out of the car." James could hear everything clearly. This was great! Jason Dowell was in charge, and the two men in the car were getting scared fast. He could tell by the looks on their faces that they had no idea what was going on, but James saw a look of desperation creeping into their expressions. They *were* carrying stolen artifacts on federal property, after all.

"Step out of the car, now." Ranger Dowell commanded. The patrol car had stopped directly in front of Red Sanders's vehicle. Even if he had wanted to make a run for it, he had nowhere to go.

As the men climbed slowly out of their car, a loud thumping began from inside the trunk. Shanda was banging on the car, screaming "Help! Help me!!" over and over.

Red Sanders stared in shock at the trunk of his own car. There was no possible explanation for how anyone could have gotten in there, and yet here was all this noise right when they were hoping to slip away, unnoticed. There was nothing to do but open the trunk. As it opened, the two law enforcement officers saw Shanda lying on top of the luggage.

"Thank you, THANK YOU so much!" Shanda screamed. "These men knew I was going to cause problems for them, and they stuffed me in here!!" *Wow,* thought James, *this performance might be good for an Oscar nomination.* Shanda appeared frantic over her situation and relieved to see help arrive. Was she crying?? *OMG, I can't believe this!*

"Officer, I've never seen this girl and I have no idea how she got in there!" Dr. Sanders's knees were shaking now. Rodney, like his boss, was totally confused by the whole situation. One minute they were driving away, and the next the police were finding a supposedly kidnapped girl in the trunk of their car.

"Look!" Shanda screamed, climbing out. "Look what they have in the trunk of this car! No wonder they wanted to keep me quiet." She pointed to the green duffel bag in the trunk, now unzipped and overflowing with the stolen artifacts.

At the sight of the stolen goods, the two officers swung into action. The driver of the patrol car immediately radioed HQ for more support, while Jason Dowell addressed the men in forceful, serious tones.

"Gentlemen, this is a serious crime we're looking at. Holding this girl against her will is bad enough. Add to that attempted theft of prehistoric federal property, and you two are looking at some serious jail time. Anything you want to tell us?"

Rodney was the first to speak. "It was his idea!" pointing at his boss. "He said it would be easy to take a few things out of the cave and we'd be rich!"

"Shut up, idiot!" Dr. Sanders had come out of his distress mode and was trying to limit the damage. "I have never seen this girl, ever! And I have no idea where this duffel bag came from."

"Yes, we have seen her!" Rodney gasped. "She's that nosy kid who was watching us in Blackall Avenue in the cave. I told you she'd be trouble!"

"That's why they grabbed me!" Shanda jumped in. "They knew I'd turn them in."

"Shanda," Ranger Dowell spoke. "Did these two men threaten to hurt you at any time?"

"No, sir, they told me they were going to keep me quiet until we got way out of the park, then give me a quarter to make a phone call. They were trying to keep me from telling you about the artifacts."

"Sir, this poor girl is delusional. We may have seen her in the cave, but I've never spoken to her at all, let alone..."

"I've heard plenty from you, sir." Officer Dowell cut Sanders off forcefully. "You've got plenty of explaining to do here."

While this scene was being played out in the parking lot, James watched a second patrol car arrive, flashers blazing. A small crowd of interested onlookers was gathering. As Sanders proclaimed his innocence and Rodney pretty much confessed to everything, two officers began to carefully lift artifacts out of the green duffel bag. They pulled out dozens of cane reed torches, several stone tools, two dried gourd fragments, and even a pair of grass moccasins.

"Gentlemen, you are under arrest for the attempted theft of priceless prehistoric artifacts from a national park. Shanda, these men are facing serious jail time as it is. Since you appear to be unharmed, would you be willing to drop the charges against them?"

If the two thieves had been thinking clearly, they would have realized right then what had happened. There was no way a teenaged girl had the right to dismiss kidnapping charges, even if she wanted to. However, they were guilty of the theft, and they knew they were done for. Kidnapping or not, they would both be in police custody for a while.

"Yes, sir," the girl replied to Jason Dowell's question. "I just don't want them to get away with trying to steal this stuff." She gestured to the stolen items.

"Don't worry about that, young lady. These two have got some serious explaining to do. I guess it will take them five to seven years or so to clear it all up."

"Five years! He did it! It was his idea!" Rodney's face was red and he started crying uncontrollably. Normally James would take pity on someone in such distress, but he couldn't find any mercy in his heart for a man who had tried to steal artifacts from the cave. Those items were national treasures.

As Richard and Courtney had explained to him more than once, Mammoth Cave was a national wonder, belonging to all Americans.

"Gentlemen, you have a right to remain silent. Anything you say can and will be used against you in a court of law. You are entitled..." *Just like on TV!* When Jason was done giving them their rights, he handcuffed his two prisoners and directed them to the back seat of his vehicle.

James couldn't control himself any longer. He sprinted across the lot to where Shanda stood. She was staring daggers at the two thieves, a look of triumphant satisfaction on her face.

"James! We did it!" she screamed. The two friends hugged and jumped up and down in their excitement. "We put them away!"

As Red Sanders was being placed in the back of the patrol car, he looked up to see that James had arrived.

"You!" The pieces all fell into place for him quickly: Shanda staring at him in the cave, catching James in his room, and Corey's insistence that they come inside for a minute before departing. "I can't believe it," he said in disgust.

"Oh, believe it, brother, believe it! You've been punked by the best!" Shanda's exuberance was contagious, and the police and the growing crowd of onlookers started laughing along with her. James was so happy he thought his chest would explode.

As the police car drove the two thieves out of the parking

lot, Red Sanders noticed Corey Chaney leaning on a post near the door, a quiet smile on his face.

Chapter XII

"For the second time in just five months, this national park owes you two a great debt of gratitude." Superintendent Thompson spoke to the two friends in front of a small gathering. The group was assembled in the meeting room at the training center. James's parents were there, along with Uncle Richard, Corey, and Aunt Courtney. Ranger Matthew was sitting next to Shanda, beaming like he had swallowed the sun. Park archaeologists and a few other rangers whom James vaguely recognized sat at different spots around the room.

"The last time we spoke, it was with mixed emotions. You had solved a great mystery, but you had acted irresponsibly in the process. The park service can never condone dangerous practices, no matter what the intended result is."

"Today is different. We are here to congratulate you on a job well done and an irreplaceable treasure recovered. James, Shanda, would you come forward please."

James heart was racing, again. *This place must be good for my circulation*, he thought idly. *My heart rate goes through the roof at least once a day.* Next to him, Shanda was glowing.

"I have contacted the Director of the National Park Service, and on behalf of the NPS, I am proud to award you two our distinguished service award."

"Sir," Shanda blurted out. "It wasn't just us. We had help from Corey and Ranger Dowell. There's no way this could have happened without them."

"I am aware of that and they know how much we appreciate everything they've done. I am also pleased that you two had the good sense to contact responsible adults, rather than get in over your heads in a potentially dangerous situation."

He means he's glad we didn't get him in trouble again.

"So thank you for including them, Shanda, but today is your day. On behalf of many grateful people at the NPS, I am proud to give you these awards."

Superintendent Thompson gave each of them a small white box. Inside were gold pins, created in the shape of the park service arrowhead. The two friends smiled awkwardly as everyone present stood and applauded for them.

The trip home was a welcome relief. James had told his parents and aunt and uncle their story several times; they couldn't help noticing that he elaborated and added a few more details of their daring deeds with each retelling. Now they were headed back to Ohio, having said goodbye to friends and family. James and Shanda were famous among the park guides, and they had received many invitations to come back soon. Ranger Joyce had even suggested they call her when they reached their eighteenth birthdays. "We can always use good people on the guide force," she had added.

"Ladies and gentlemen, behold the Rotunda! The site where African slaves were forced to dig cave dirt for twelve hours a day to protect America's liberty!" I could do that, James thought happily.

As they drove down the big hill toward Cincinnati, his cell phone beeped. A picture of a panda bear appeared on his screen: text from Shanda.

"Turn round, QUICK! Some1 has stolen the cave!"

"Jas and Shnda detective agency, on it."

"YOU MEAN SHNDA & JAS AGCY!"

"How bout Rattlesnake Investigations?"

"U got it! C U next summer, snake boy!"

Distinguished Service Award

Presented to

Shanda and James

for Outstanding Service and Dedication
to the National Park Service

Affirmed on this day October 10th

Patrick Martin
National Park Superintendent

APPENDIX

Although the adventures of James and Shanda are fictional, the artifacts left behind by native people in Mammoth Cave are very real.

Archaeologists tell us that people moved into the Mammoth Cave area as early as fourteen thousand years ago, during the Paleo-Indian period. These tribes were hunter-gatherers, who survived off wild plants and game.

As people developed better tools and weapons, their lifestyles changed. Around eight thousand years ago, during the archaic period, they began to move into river valleys and establish primitive agriculture. Sunflowers, squash, and sumpweed were among their earliest crops. Starting about four thousand years ago, a wild plant known as chenopod was grown for grain,.

Archaeologists call the period from 1000 BC to 900 AD the woodland period. This era is characterized by farming on a larger scale. People settled into larger villages and were able to store food for the winter. As they settled, other tribes

Steve Kistler

occasionally attacked them to steal their resources. Settlements were protected by walls and new weapons were developed. It was during this era that the bow and arrow was invented.

Native people used Mammoth Cave extensively from about 2000 BC to around the year 0. They extracted large amounts of a white mineral, called gypsum. Today we can only guess at what they used it for. Gypsum forms a base for a plaster-like substance, as well as a type of paint. It can be used to preserve meat. It is often found with other salty minerals on the cave walls.

Whatever their uses for gypsum, these people traded extensively. In local archaeological sites, we find buffalo horns from Montana and shells from the Atlantic coast. Adding to the mystery is this fact: gypsum dissolves completely when it gets wet. We don't find any remains of this mineral outside the dry cave. However, we can see that many tons of gypsum were removed from Mammoth and nearby caves.

Visitors to Mammoth Cave who are interested in Native American artifacts should consider taking the Violet City Lantern Tour. This three-mile tour takes one deep into the cave, where old torches and primitive artwork can still be found today.